# Wallace & Gromit™
# ANORAKNOPHOBIA

Story and Text by
## Tristan Davies
Drawings by
## Nick Newman

Hodder & Stoughton

Lettering by Gary Gilbert

Additional colouring by
Tony Trimmer and Fiona Newman

First published in Great Britain in 1998 by Hodder & Stoughton
A division of Hodder Headline PLC

10 9 8 7 6 5 4 3 2 1

A CIP catalogue record for this title is available from the British Library

ISBN 0 8417 2031 2

Printed by Jarrolds Book Printing, Norfolk

Published in the United States
Distribooks Inc.
8120 N. Ridgeway
SKOKIE, IL. 60076
Tel. (847) 676-1596
Toll free Fax (888) 266-5713

# Wallace & Gromit™
# ANORAKNOPHOBIA

### WALLACE
Inventor of the ground- (and furniture) breaking Ping-Pong-O-Matic Automated Home Leisure System who, under hypnosis, learns what it's like to lead a dog's life.

### GROMIT
A dog already so busy leading a dog's life (washing the socks, ironing the milk cartons, polishing the Tupperware, etc) he has little time for Home Leisure — even if it is Automated.

### MR PATEL
Pigeon fancier and expert on prevailing wind conditions, Wallace's nextdoor neighbour is very interested in, er, wind and pigeons.

### DEREK
A game old carrier pigeon and Mr Patel's absolutely favouritest bird.

### MR DO IT ALL
Doorman, receptionist, porter, bell boy, gardener and barman at the Hotel Splendio on the Northern Riviera.
(It's a job share.)

### THE HERR DOKTOR COUNT BARON NAPOLEON VON STRUDEL, *aka* BERT MAUDSLEY
Dastardly founder of the Acme Corporation and inventor of the Acme Utility Anorak, he has a surprise up his sleeve and something even yukkier behind his eye patch.

### THE CONTESSA BARONESS MADAME FRAULEIN QUEENIE VON STRUDEL, *aka* QUEENIE MAUDSLEY
Whip-cracking variety artiste whose arachnid trapeze act has mesmerised audiences from Berlin to Barnoldswick — and sometimes all the way back again.

### CLEETHORPES and CLITHEROE
Bert and Queenie's polite, erudite twins, whose hobbies are pressing dried flowers and translating the mystical writings of Thomas à Kempis back into Latin.
OR: Two complete and utter nutters. (Delete where applicable.)

### DEREK, DERRICK AND ERIC
Gentleman inventors and exhibitionists, who for the purposes of this story are making an exhibition of themselves at an Acme Corporation-sponsored Invention Convention.

### THE SPIDERS FROM MARGATE
A troupe of performing arachnids from Margate and the surrounding area (although one, it's true, was brought up by an aunt in Folkestone).

I AY, OMIT. ANCY A AME O' ABLE ENNIS?

ANGRY RUSTLE!

ANGRY RUSTLE!

INVENTOR'S CHRONICLE

I 'AID...

FANCY A GAME OF TABLE TENNIS?

OR DARTS?

OR BILLIARDS EVEN?

IF MY PING PONG-O-MATIC WITH ALL THE TRIMMINGS IS A HIT, THE FAST-MOVING WORLD OF AUTOMATED INDOOR LEISURE COULD BE ... OUR OYSTER!

SO WILL YOU BE ME GUINEA PIG THEN?

HMM. LOOKS LIKE I'LL HAVE TO DO FIELD TRIALS MYSELF.

BETTER GET YER SKATES ON!

WE DON'T WANT A REPEAT OF LAST WASHDAY.

IF YOU NEED ME, I'LL BE... TINKERING WITH ME TRAJECTORIES!

EE BAH GUM, OUR GROMIT. THAT'S A CRACKIN' SIGHT THAT IS!

PIGEONS! COMING HOME TO ROOST. IN FORMATION!

NOT THAT YER ADULT BLUE-GREY *COLUMBINA LIVIA* WITH TRADEMARK LILAC NECK PATCH DOES THAT OFF ITS OWN BAT. OH NO.

TRAINED 'EM MESELF, I DID. EE BAH GUM!

H-E-L-P! THE PING PONG-O-MATIC'S MALFUNCTIONING!

WHIZZ!

WHOOSH!

DUCK, GROMIT, DUCK!!!

DUCK!! WHERE??

WHIZZ!

WHOOSH!

WHIZZ! FIZZ! WHOOSH!

ER, I'LL SWITCH THE MACHINE BACK TO TABLE TENNIS MODE.

THUD! THWACK! THWANG-G-G!

SORRY!!

SQUELCH!

SORRY...

...YOU'D BETTER PULL YER STORM COVER UP LAD...

...THEY'RE COMIN' IN THICK AND SQUELCHY NOW! EE BAH GUM!

HEAVE! TUG! SQUEAK! YANK!

PING! POING! PING! POING!

SPLOSH! SPLASH! SPLASH!

PEDAL FASTER, LAD!

PULL HARDER, LAD!

IT'S NO USE, GROMIT. YOU'LL JUST HAVE TO WASH THE WHOLE LOT AGAIN.

I RECKON I'M DONE NOW, CHUCK.

SO IF YOU'LL JUST WALK THIS WAY, I'VE A SURPRISE ...

DA DAA! *TWO* PING-PONG-O-MATIC AUTOMATIC HOME LEISURE SYSTEMS!! WHICH MEANS YOU ONLY NEED *ONE* PERSON...

...FOR A GAME OF DOUBLES!

SO LONG AS YOU'VE REMEMBERED TO SECURE THE TEAPOT, THAT IS.

WHICH I HAVE!

BANG!

'COURSE THERE'S ALWAYS DARTS MODE...

...BUT I FANCY A RUBBER OF TABLE TENNIS.

SO CRANK THE HANDLES, LAD -- AND STAND BACK!

CRANK! WIND!

PLAY!!

WHIZZ! BOING! BOING! WHIZZ!

WOBBLE! WOBBLE!

JOLT! JOLT!

FUNNY! THE R-ROOM'S NOT S-SUPPOSED TO V-V-VIBRATE LIKE TH-THIS! *H-E-L-P!*

D-O-O-O-O SOMETHING, GROMIT! IT'S NOT THE PING PONG-O-MATIC THAT'S MALFUNCTIONING...

... THE VIBRATIONS ARE COMING FROM THE ...

J-JUDDER! J-JUDDER!

WE EEM OO AV AD A IT O OTHER ...

I SAID: WE SEEM TO HAVE HAD A BIT OF BOTHER IN THE LAUNDER-AMA DEPARTMENT.

AND NO WONDER IF THAT'S WHERE ME BILLIARD BALLS WENT.

NOW WE'RE SNOOKERED. WE'LL NEVER REPAIR THIS DRUM -- AND WE CERTAINLY CAN'T AFFORD A REPLACEMENT.

ANY IDEAS, LAD?

IN CO... ...ION ...ION
FIRST PRIZE £100-

TAP! TAP!

SEVERAL HOURS LATER...

THERE. IF WE'RE QUICK WE'LL JUST CATCH THE LAST PIGEON POST.

Acme Corp
P.O. Box 666
England

DEREK!

RUN THIS TO THE POST BOX WILL YOU, CHUCK? APPLICATIONS CLOSE TOMORROW -- AND GROMIT AND ME NEED THE PRIZE MONEY!

SOME DAYS LATER...

AH! CORRESPONDENCE. I SHALL ATTEND TO IT IN THE STUDY.

THUMP! BANG!

WONDER IF THERE'S ANY WORD FROM THE INVENTION CONVENTION PEOPLE?

GREAT NEWS! THE ACME CORPORATION HAS SEEN MY DESIGNS FOR THE PING PONG-O-MATIC AND WE'VE BEEN INVITED TO BECOME ... EXHIBITIONISTS!

YOU'D BETTER FINISH YER BREAKFAST AND GET AN EARLY NIGHT. YOU'VE A TIRING DAY AHEAD OF US TOMORROW.

EARLY NEXT MORNING...

IT'S ALL CLEAR, LAD. ME PIGEONS WON'T BE BACK 'TIL DINNER TIME...

...NOT UNLESS THE PREVAILING NORTH-EASTERLY FORCE 6 GUSTING 7 BECOMES A FRESH SOUTH-WESTERLY 8 TO 9 ...

... IN WHICH CASE THEY'LL BE -- LOOK OUT, GROMIT!

SPLASH!

SPLASH!

LATER...

NO PARKING GARAGE IN CONSTANT USE

HEAVE!

PANT! SWEAT!

AND LATER STILL...

RECKON YOUR SIDECAR MUST BE FULL BY NOW.

JO PARKING GARAGE CONSTANT USE

DOG BISCUITS

OH, WE'RE THROUGH WITH THE INTERNAL COMBUSTION ENGINE AND TRADITIONAL HORSEPOWER.

FROM NOW ON IT'S DOGPOWER! PEDAL ON, LAD, PEDAL ON!

WAL 2

8

9

NOW WE'RE UP THE CREEK WITHOUT A LEG TO STAND ON.

BETTER GET PADDLING.

C'MON LAD. GIVE IT SOME WELLY.

LESS WELLY-GLUG-GLUG-GLUG!

I CAN'T ATTEND THE INVENTION CONVENTION WITH ME TANK TOP COVERED IN SLIME.

HOPE THERE'S TIME TO GET IT LAUNDERED BEFORE I MEET MY FELLOW PIONEERS OF PROGRESS.

ON THE NORTHERN RIVIERA...

TWINNED WITH GRIMSVILLE SUR MER

SLACKEN OFF, LAD. WE'LL FREEWHEEL THE LAST BIT.

HOTEL SPLENDI O**

BLIMEY! THIS LOOKS POSITIVELY, ER, SPLENDIO.

OH NO! IT'S THOSE ROAD HOGS AGAIN. REMIND ME TO KEEP THE BATH PLUG IN -- WE DON'T WANT 'EM GETTING IN OUR ENSUITE FACILITIES.

CAUTION LIVE SPIDERS

WELCOME TO THE HOTEL SPLENDIO, SIR -- JEWEL OF THE NORTHERN RIVIERA!

HOTEL

WELC ME

CAN I INTEREST SIR IN OUR PERSONALISED VALET PARKING SERVICE?

NO THANKS. WE TRIED PARKING IN YOUR VALLEY -- AND VERY SQUELCHY IT WAS TOO.

PONG-

O-MATIC

PARTS

BUT I COULD MURDER A WASH AND BRUSH UP.

VERY GOOD, SIR. IF YOU GO TO RECEPTION THE MANAGER WILL SEE YOU SHORTLY.

TWENTY MINUTES LATER...

PRIVATE

INVENTION CONVENTION COCKTAIL PARTY 7.30 IN THE BANQUETING HALL

TWENTY MORE MINUTES LATER...

SERVICE SEEMS A LITTLE ON THE NON-EXISTENT SIDE.

BRRRING!

BRRRING!

WELCOME TO THE HOTEL SPLENDIO, SIR -- PANT! PANT! -- JEWEL OF THE NORTHERN RIVIERA!

FOR THE COMFORT OF OTHER GUESTS ATTENDING THE INVENTION CONVENTION, WE WOULD ASK YOU TO REFRAIN FROM USING POWER TOOLS IN THE OCEANSIDE BUTTERY RESTAURANT BEFORE 9AM.

AND IN THE MORNING, WILL SIR BE REQUIRING A COMPLIMENTARY...

...NEWSPAPER?

NEWSPAPER!? I HOPE NOT. OUR GROMIT'S HOUSE-TRAINED, YOU KNOW. AND BESIDE'S, WE'VE GOT EN-SUITE FACILITIES.

PRIVATE

PING PONG-

O-MATIC

PARTS

THEN IF YOU'LL JUST FOLLOW ME TO THE LIFT...

PING PONG

THIS WAY UP

O-MATIC

PARTS

FLIPPIN' 'ECK!!!

PING PONG-

O-MATIC

LOOKS LIKE YOU'LL HAVE TO TAKE THE STAIRS. BUT DON'T WORRY -- IT'S ONLY AN EIGHT-FLOOR WALK-UP!

MIND THE PAINTWORK! WE ONLY 'AD IT DONE IN '57!

WILL THAT BE ALL, SIR? AHEM, AHEM!

ER, CAN YOU JUST TELL ME HOW TO CONTACT ROOM SERVICE?

EASY. DIAL 9. FOLLOWED BY THE SUM OF THE TWO DIGITS OF YER ROOM NUMBER. MINUS THE NUMBER OF NIGHTS YOU'RE STAYING. DIVIDED BY WHAT FLOOR YER ON. AHEM AHEM!

ER, HOW D'YOU DO? MY NAME IS WALLACE. PEOPLE CALL ME...WALLACE.

ER, DELIGHTED. WILL THERE BE OWT ELSE?

OO. YOU COULD TAKE ME TANK TOP TO THE LAUNDRY. WE'VE GOT COCKTAILS AT HALF PAST SEVEN AND I WANT TO LOOK ME BEST.

AND ME SHOES AND SOCKS COULD DO WITH A ONCE OVER, AN' ALL.

FORTY WINKS LATER...

ZZZZ!

COO-COO!
COO-COO!

DON'T PANIC, LAD. IT'S NOT REAL PIGEONS...

ONLY MR PATEL'S COO-COO CLOCK.

NOW WHAT'S HAPPENED TO MY LAUNDRY?

I MUST BE PROPERLY ATTIRED FOR THE CONVENTION. BETTER RING DOWN.

FUNNY... THE LINE'S DEAD!

14

PING PONG—  O-MATIC

CLUMP CLUMP!  CLUMP CLUMP!

CLUMP CLUMP!  CLUMP CLUMP!

CLUMP CLUMP CLUMP CLUMP!!

CLUMP! CLUMP!  SERVICE LIFT  OUT OF ORDER

OUT OF ORDER  NIMBLE LEAP!

MEANWHILE, WALLACE IS STILL LOOKING FOR HIS WASHING...

HMM. THE SERVICE ISN'T GETTING ANY BETTER.

DRUM! DRUM!

PRIVATE

I SAY... HELLO... ANYONE AT HOME? COO-EE?

PRIVATE

COO-ERR! TALK ABOUT SECURITY-CONSCIOUS...

SLAM!

OI! LET ME OUT!! I'M WITH THE INVENTION CONVENTION-- I'M ONE OF THE EXHIBITIONISTS !!!!

CLUNK! CLICK!

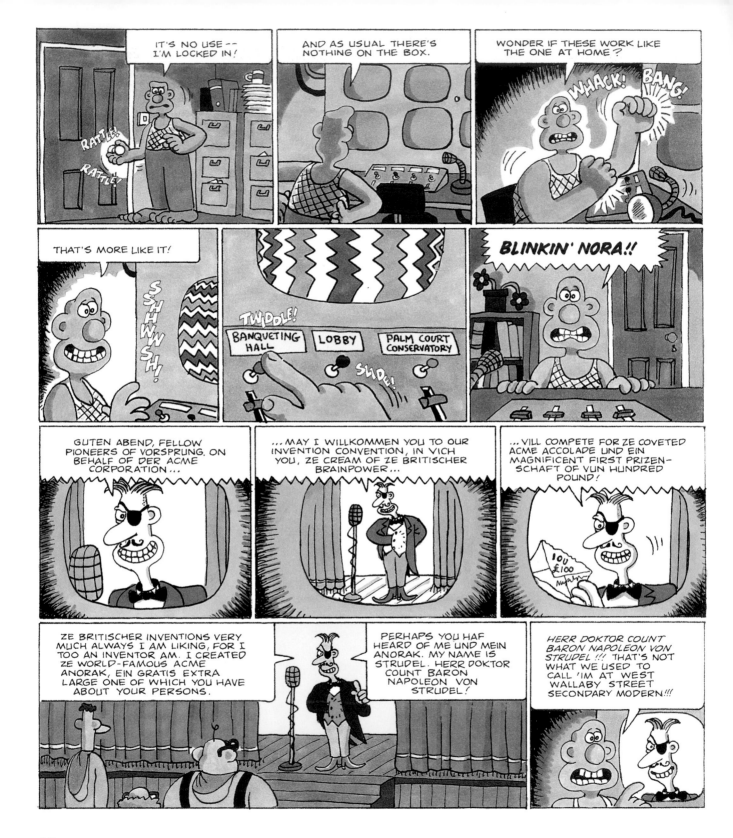

BEFORE VEE ZE INVENTION CONVENTION PROPER BEGINNING ARE...

BACK IN DER BANQUETING HALL...

... EINE KLEINE NACHTMUSIK UND TOP FLIGHT EVENING'S ENTERTAINMENT THE ACME CORPORATION PROPOSING IS.

REMEMBER-- VE HAF VAYS OF MAKING YOU ENJOY YOURSELF! AND YOU *VILL* ENJOY ZIS INTERNATIONAL CABARET ARTISTE...

...WHO'S SPELLBOUND AUDIENCES FROM BERLIN TO YOUR OWN DEAR BARNOLDSWICK LADIES UND DAMEN--

THE CONTESSA BARONESS MADAME FRAULEIN...QUEENIE VON STRUDEL!!!

...UND ZE SPIDERS FROM MARGATE!!!

CANNED APPLAUSE!

WHAT D'YA RECKON, ERIC?

DUNNO, DERRICK. WHAT DOES DEREK THINK?

SHE'S...A BIG LASS!

KERRACK!

SPIDERS ASCEND-- AND PREPARE TO SPIN!!!

KERRACK!

SPIDERS STEADY --AND PREPARE TO SWING!!!

BACK IN THE SECURITY ROOM...

VORSPRUNG DURCH TECHNIK! FORGET THE FLOORSHOW-- THAT'S MY PING PONG-O-MATIC THEY'VE PINCHED!

CLEETHORPES! CLITHEROE!

YES, MAM?

GET THESE THREE ANORAKED -- NOW!!!

YES, MAM.

SPIDERS DESCEND!!!

AND PREPARE TO WEAVE!!!

AS FOR YOU BERT MAUDSLEY...

OPERATION S.P.A.R.R.O.W. CAN'T AFFORD ANY MORE OF YOUR SLIP OOPS!

SO CRANK OOP THE PING PONG-O-MATIC -- AND STICK IT ON DARTS MODE IN CASE THE INVENTORS TRY TO ESCAPE!!!

ANYTHING YOU SAY, PET.

CLEETHORPES! CLITHEROE! QUIT SCRAPPIN' NOW!!!

IF IT'S A FIGHT YOU WANT, FETCH ME WALLACE -- DEAD OR ALIVE!!!

BACK IN THE SECURITY ROOM...

TWIN PIQUES! HERE COMES TROUBLE...

YES, MAM.

AWW! THANKS MAM!

21

'E'S GETTING AWAY! OUR MAM'LL BRAIN US!!

SERVICE LIFT

'S ALL RIGHT. I'VE GORRANIDEA. WE'LL GO AFTER 'IM!

FASTER, LAD! THIS INVENTION CONVENTION'S TURNING NASTY. THEY'VE ONLY PURLOINED MY PING PONG-O-MATIC FOR PURPOSES OF A CRIMINAL NATURE!

CRASH! JOLT!

JUDDER!

IS THE COAST CLEAR?

SERVICE LIFT

OUT OF ORDER

CLEARLY NOT! GRAB THAT SERVICE TROLLEY, LAD!

SERVICE LI

I DON'T KNOW WHAT THE SPEED LIMIT IS IN HOTEL CORRIDORS-- BUT FEEL FREE TO GIVE IT SOME WELLY!!!

HANG ABOUT! LET'S SEE IF WE CAN'T GET THE TWINS INTO A LATHER!

COURTESY BUBBLE BATH

BFF!

COURTESY BUBBLE BATH

SPIT!

COURTESY BUBBLE BATH

EXCELLENT! OUR ESCAPE'S ASSURED SO LONG AS NO ONE'S BEEN SILLY ENOUGH TO LEAVE ANYTHING LYING AROUND LIKE--

GLUG! GLUG!

A COMPACT VACUUM CLEANER!!!

AAAARRGGHHHH!!!

FIRE POINT

THWACK!

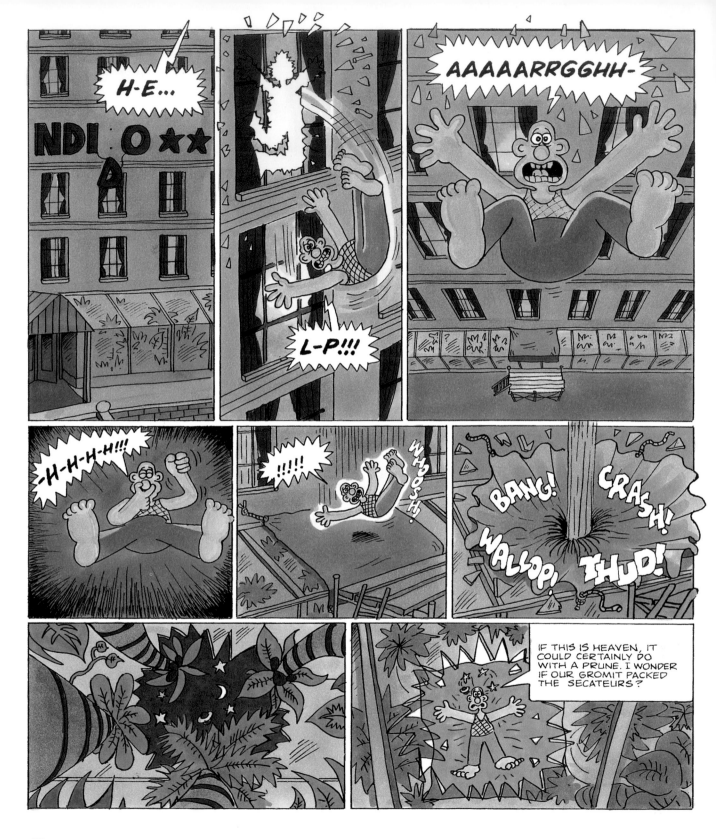

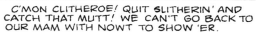

RIGHT PAW DOWN A BIT -- OR YOU'LL MISS THE RUNWAY!

*RIGHT!* WITH THE PING PONG-O-MATIC STOLEN, ME LAUNDRY MISSING AND OUR FELLOW INVENTORS BEING BRAINWASHED IN THE BANQUETING HALL, THIS IS *WAR!*

PREPARE FOR JUNGLE COMBAT, GROMIT!

I ALSO THINK IT'S TIME WE ALERTED THE HOTEL AUTHORITIES TO WHAT'S GOING ON IN THEIR ESTABLISHMENT.

HELLO! THERE'S THE SPLENDIO'S DOORMAN, RECEPTIONIST, PORTER, ROOM SERVICE OPERATIVE, LAUNDRY-MAN AND GARDENER NOW.

EXCUSE ME! MR DO-IT-ALL! I'D LIKE TO LODGE A COMPLAINT!

ER... WELCOME TO THE HOTEL SPLENDIO, SIR, JEWEL OF THE NORTHERN RIVIERA. WE HOPE YOU...

WHERE'S MY BLINKIN' WASHING?

UM... ER...

YOU'LL NOT BE NEEDING ANY NEW TANK TOPS WHEN I'VE FINISHED WITH YA, WALLACE !!!

DON'T MOVE! I'VE GOT YOU COVERED BY ONE OF YER OWN INVENTIONS -- AND AS YOU KNOW IT MIGHT GO HAYWIRE AT ANY MINUTE.

HELLO, QUEENIE. HELLO BERT. IT'S BEEN A LONG TIME SINCE YOU AND THE SPARROW STREET GANG USED TO CHASE ME HOME FROM SCHOOL.

'APPEN. BUT YOU WON'T ESCAPE THIS TIME. NOT ONCE YOU'VE UNDERGONE NEURO-LINGUISTIC TRANSMOGRIFICATION WITH T'OTHER INVENTORS!

PSST! THINK IT'S TIME WE SCARPERED. WHEN I SAY 'NOW', ER ... SCARPER!

QUIT WHISPERING WHEN I'M YELLIN' AT YA!

ER...

NOW!

OI! I'LL TEACH YA TO RUN OUT ON QUEENIE MAUDSLEY!

I WEREN'T DISQUALIFIED AS WEST WALLABY STREET SECONDARY MODERN'S JAVELIN CHAMPION THREE YEARS RUNNIN' FOR NOWT, YA KNOW!!

SHEEOOO!

SHEEOOO!  CRASH!  SPRAWL!

THWANGGG!

WE MUST STOP 'EM REACHING THE OTHERS IN THE BANQUETING HALL: THE HYPNOSIS ISN'T COMPLETE!

CRANK MY HANDLE, BERT MAUDSLEY!!

WITH THE PING PONG-O-MATIC IN BILLIARD MODE, WE'LL MAKE SURE THE PALM COURT CONSERVATORY'S PANORAMIC SEA VIEW IS THE LAST THING THEY SEE!

CRANK! WIND!

ANYTHING YOU SAY, PETAL!

BY 'ECK! DID SHE REALLY GO TO THE SAME SCHOOL AS YOU?

SHE DID UNTIL SHE WERE EXPELLED AFTER THE INCIDENT WITH THE HEADMASTER AND THE BUNSEN BURNER!

WHIZZ! FIZZ! WHIZZ!

G-DOING! G-DOING! G-DOING!

ER, MUCH AS I'M ENJOYING TALKING TO YOU AS PART OF THE HOTEL SPLENDIO'S ONGOING COMMITMENT TO CUSTOMER CARE...

...IT'S TIME I MADE A RUN FOR IT AND OPENED THE ANGRY LOBSTER...

... WHICH OFFERS A FULL SELECTION OF BAR SNACKS AND SWEETS FROM THE HOSTESS TROLLEY-- DO POP IN IF YOU'RE PASSING!

YOU'RE NOT POPPIN' NOWHERE, WALLACE!

NOT BEFORE I TEACH YOU A LESSON YOU SHOULDA LEARNT IN SCHOOL.

CRANK MY HANDLE ONE MORE TIME, OUR BERT!

ANYTHING YOU SAY, MY SUGAR PLUM FAIRY!

AND WE'LL SHOW 'IM THERES NO SUCH THING AS A GLASS CEILING FOR A CAREER WOMAN LIKE ME! HA HA!!

CRASH! SHATTER! SMASH!

BAREFOOT CONTESSAS, GROMIT! WE'RE AT THE SHARP END OF A GIRL POWER SANDWICH AND NO MISTAKE!

HA! LOOK AT 'IM NOW, BERT. WEST WALLABY STREET SECONDARY MODERN'S TABLE TENNIS CHAMP-- BEATEN BY 'IS OWN PING PONG-O-MATIC!

ER, WHEN I SAY...

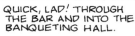

...'JUMP ON ME BACK, GROMIT'... JUMP ON ME BACK.

ER...'JUMP ON ME BACK, GROMIT'.

COME BACK 'ERE OR I'LL-- OUCH! OUCH!

TINKLE!

SCRUNCH!

CRUNCH!

QUICK, LAD! THROUGH THE BAR AND INTO THE BANQUETING HALL.

ANGRY LOBSTER BAR

THE OTHER INVENTORS'LL BECOME ACME'S ACOLYTES IF WE CAN'T HALT THE HYPNOSIS!

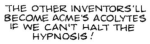

RY ER R

LET ME IN, NOW!

ER, I AGREE!

SLAM!

JAM!

AH! GOOD EVENING! WELCOME TO THE ANGRY LOBSTER, GASTRONOMIC EPI-CENTRE OF THE HOTEL SPLENDIO ...

...AND HOME TO THE FINEST SELECTION OF FROZEN BAR SNACKS ON THE NORTHERN RIVIERA!

NO TIME FOR THAT! CALL THE POLICE AND TELL THEM CALMLY YOUR HOTEL'S CRIMINAL FAMILY THE MAUDSLEYS OVER TAKEN BY BEEN HAS !!

AND MAKE IT SNIPPY!

PUSH!

AARGHH!

HELP, GROMIT! I'M GOING DOWN WITH A SEVERE CASE OF ARACHNOPHOBIA !!!

AW, PLEASE CAN WE WATCH, OUR MAM?

DOG FISH

PLEASE CAN WE SEE HOW YA DO IT?

BUT SIR HASN'T MADE HIS SELECTION FROM THE HOSTESS TROLLEY!

SPRIN!

GROMIT RACES TO RECEPTION ...

PRIVATE

... AND INTO THE SECURITY ROOM.

SHW SHW SHHH!

BUT YOU'VE GOT ME PING PONG-O-MATIC ...

IN THE BANQUETING HALL ...

WHY CAN'T YOU LET ME GO?

TOO LATE! YOU'VE SEEN TOO MUCH OF OUR WORK AT THE ACME CORPORATION AND OF ... OPERATION S.P.A.R.R.O.W!

OUR ONGOING OPERATION TO STEAL, PILFER AND RECKLESSLY REQUISITION ...

OTHER PEOPLE'S WORK!

TO COMPENSATE ME FOR THE THEFT OF MY OWN UNIQUE INVENTION, THE ACME UTILITY ANORAK ...

...WHICH HAS BEEN PLAGIARISED, PILLORIED AND NOW POPULAR-ISED THE WORLD OVER WITH NO DUE DESIGN ROYALTY PAYABLE TO YOURS TRULY!

BUT YOUR OPERATION DOESN'T ADD UP.

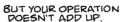

WHY NOT?

YOU CAN'T STEAL, PILFER AND RECKLESSLY REQUISITION OTHER PEOPLES WORK IF THERE'S ONLY ONE 'P' IN 'SPARROW'.

YOU KNOW WE WERE TOO POOR TO AFFORD SPELLING IN OUR HOUSE! BUT ENOUGH! QUEENIE: START THE SPECIAL HYPNOSIS!!

IT'LL BE A PLEASURE PET! YOU KNOW HOW I'VE ALWAYS WANTED A POODLE OF ME OWN !!!

SPIDERS, DESCEND!

NOW WATCH ME HAIRY BEAUTIES, WALLACE. AND LISTEN ONLY TO MY VOICE!

YOU ARE FEELING RELAXED...

...RELAXED AND SLEEPY...

...AS SLEEPY AS THE DOZIEST INVENTOR WHAT WAS EVER INVENTED!

AND AS YOU CLOSE YOUR EYES, IMAGINE A STEEP STAIRCASE BEFORE YOU.

A STAIRCASE YOU BEGIN TO DESCEND, ONE STEP AFTER ANOTHER.

THAT'S IT. DOWN YOU GO, STEP BY STEP...

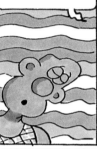

LOWER AND LOWER 'TIL YOU REACH THE BOTTOM.

AND AT THE BOTTOM OF THESE IMAGINARY STAIRS YOU SEE WALLACE'S SPECIAL NEW HOME...

SO THAT WHEN I CLICK MY FINGERS...

CLICK!

YOU LEAP INTO YER NEW DOG BASKET!!!

WOOF! WOOF!

HAHAHAHAHAHAHA!!!

WOOF! WOOF!

OW-OWWW!!

MEANWHILE AT SECURITY...

OW-OWWWWW!!

MOAN! WHIMPER!

THUMP! SIGH!

BUT MAM! WHERE'S 'E REALLY GOIN' TO SLEEP? WE 'AVEN'T GOT A KENNEL.

SHUT IT, YOU TWO! HE'LL KIP IN THE CARAVAN WI' US!

GRATEFUL PANT! DRIBBLE!

31

OW- OWWWWWW!!!

OBEDIENT STARE!

STAGE HYPNOSIS WITH QUEENIE MAUDSLEY

BREAKING TRANCES IN EMERGENCIES

AS I WAS SAYING, THERE'S ONLY ONE 'P' IN...

CHCK!

GROMIT!!

BY 'ECK IT'S A DOG'S LIFE BEING A DOG!

WE'VE GOT TO GET HELP BEFORE SOMETHING IRREVERSIBLE HAPPENS!

SPLOSH!

DEREK! ARE WE GLAD TO SEE YOU!

WE ARE IF YOU CAN GET A MESSAGE TO MR PATEL. THE INVENTION CONVENTION'S TURNED NASTY AND WE NEED BACK-UP.

RUSTLE!

RUSTLE!

STAGE HYPNOSIS WITH QUEENIE MAUDSLEY

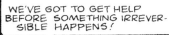

HOTEL SPLENDIO

TEAR! RIP! TEAR!

WELL DONE, GROMIT! VERY CANNILY CANINE!

HOTEL SPLENDIO

LET'S HOPE THE WIND'S BEHIND DEREK AND NOT THE OTHER WAY ROUND AS USUAL.

PIGEON EXPRESS

STUCK UP HERE THERE'S NOTHING WE CAN DO...

...BUT WAIT 'TIL WE'RE RESCUED...

..OR R-RECAPTURED!

RUN FOR IT, LAD-- ME ARACHNOPHOBIA'S COMING BACK!!!

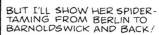

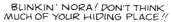

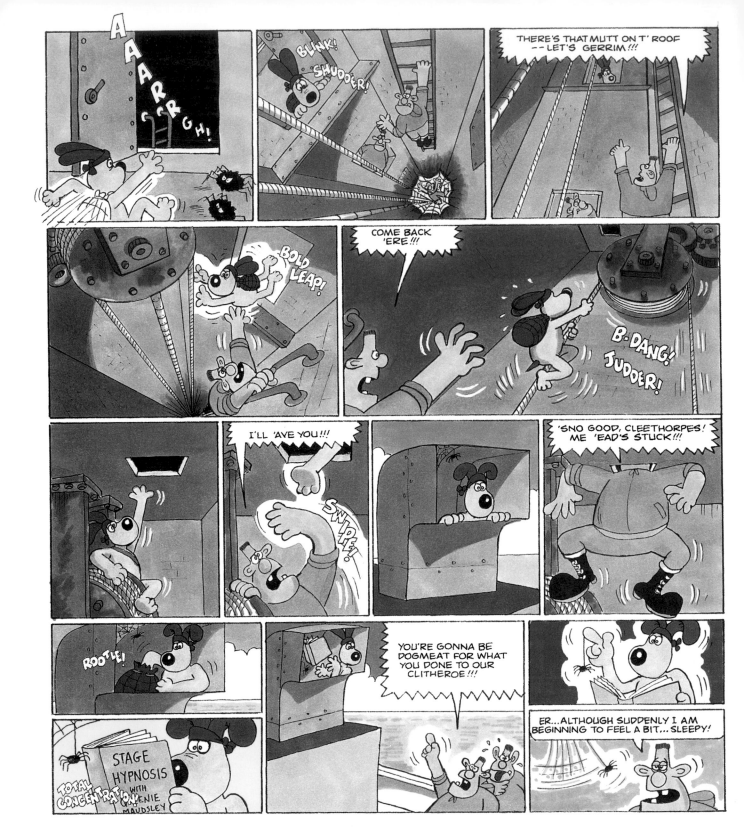

ERRR...

ERRR...

MEANWHILE, INSIDE THE HOTEL SPLENDIO...

HERE HE IS TRUSSED UP LIKE A FERRET AT EASTER!

BUT IT LOOKS LIKE THE TRANCE'S WORN OFF.

WE'LL HAVE TO THINK OF SOMETHING MORE FINAL FOR THE INVENTOR OF THE PING PONG-O-MATIC. BACK TO THE BANQUETING HALL.

RIGHT BERT MAUDSLEY, RUNNER-UP IN THE WEST WALLABY STREET SECONDARY MODERN TABLE TENNIS CHAMPIONSHIPS THREE YEARS RUNNIN'.

SHOW WALLACE WHAT YER MADE OF NOW!

IT'LL BE A PLEASURE, BLOSSOM!

YOU SEE, WALLACE. I'M NOT JUST A PRETTY FACE ALONG WITH THE ACME ANORAK, I'M THE BRAINS BEHIND...

...THE ACME TABLE TENNIS TERROR! THE WORLD'S FIRST SMART PING PONG BALL!

SQUELCH!

FITTED WITH IT'S OWN HIGHLY UNSTABLE MERCURY SWITCH INERTIA GYROSCOPE LINKED TO A SMALL EXPLOSIVE DEVICE!

SPLODGE!

DRIP!

READY FOR A MATCH, WALLACE--OR DO YOU ONLY EVER PLAY AGAINST DOGS?

CLICK!

SO THAT'S WHY YOU WANT THE PING PONG-O-MATIC -- TO LAUNCH YOUR EXPLODING SMART BALL. INDOOR LEISURE HAS DONE NOTHING TO DESERVE THIS, BERT MAUDSLEY! YOU'RE EVIL!

SHUT IT, WALLACE! SHOW 'IM WARRELSE YOU'VE GORRUP YER SLEVE, OUR BERT!

YOU MEAN SHOW HIM...

...MY TITANIUM-RIVETED, PLATINUM-PLATED...

...ACME SMART BAT, WHICH IS TUNED TO THE SAME EVIL RADIO FREQUENCY AS THE BALL!

BLINKIN' NORA!

WITH THIS I'M... *INVINCIBLE AT PING PONG!*

IS THE DEADLIEST SMART BALL ARMED, LAMBKIN?

'TIS NOW, OH MIGHTY ONE!

CLICK!

THEN *PLAY!* AND REMEMBER: THE BALL EXPLODES INSTANTLY YOU MISS A SHOT...

...IF ITS MAGNETIC MEMORY TOUCHES SO MUCH AS A BLADE OF GRASS ON THE EARTH'S SURFACE.

NOTHING CONCENTRATES THE MIND LIKE PING PONG TO THE DEATH, EH WALLACE?

THE WORLD'S PARIAH TABLE TENNIS COACHES WILL PAY HANDSOMELY FOR THE SMART BALL.

ESPECIALLY WHEN LAUNCHED FROM YOUR OWN RAPID FIRE PING PONG-O-MATIC!

NOTHING IN THE RULES ABOUT NOT OPENING THE WINDOW IS THERE?

YOU BLITHERING IDIOT!!

OH NO!!!

*LOOK OUT MISSUS!* THERE'S A HIGHLY UNSTABLE TABLE TENNIS TRAINING DEVICE HEADING STRAIGHT FOR YOU!

HOTEL SPLEN-DI-D O

40

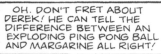
WHATEVER YOU DO, DEREK, DON'T EAT IT--

OH. DON'T FRET ABOUT DEREK! HE CAN TELL THE DIFFERENCE BETWEEN AN EXPLODING PING PONG BALL AND MARGARINE ALL RIGHT!

KERR-BANG!

WELL HE CAN NOW!

SO WHAT'S THE TROUBLE? I'D HAVE GOT HERE SOONER...

...ONLY I WERE CYCLING INTO A NORTH-WESTERLY FORCE 6 GUSTING 7 TO 8 ON THE EXPOSED PASSES OVER 2,000 FT!

BUT YOU DID CALL THE POLICE?

OH NO. I'M SURE THIS IS NOWT ME AND ME BIRDS CAN'T HANDLE! TRAINED 'EM MESELF!

CHARGE!!

DARTS, GROMIT! DUCK!!!

DUCK? WHY CERTAINLY!

WHOO-WHHT!

QUACK! QUACK! QUACK!

QUACK! QUACK!

Y-E-E-E-OW!

H-E-E-E-L-P! WHERE ARE THEM TWINS WHEN WE NEED 'EM?

FLAP! DAKA DAKA! FLAP!

YES. WHERE ARE THEY, GROMIT-- AND HOW DID YOU EVADE THEM ON THE ROOF?

HYPNOTIC STARE! LOUD CLICK!

HMM. SEEMS AN OLD DOG CAN LEARN NEW TRICKS AFTER ALL.

STAGE HYPNOSIS WITH QUEENIE MAUDSLEY

I'D BETTER LOOK FOR DEREK. WIND'S CHANGED AND HE'S BEAK-ON TO AN EASTERLY FORCE 7, GUSTING 8.

YOU CARRY ON: WE'RE ABOUT TO TRY OUT OUR FREE ACME ANORAKS!

NO! PLEEASE! NOT OUR OWN EXTRA LARGE UTILITY GARMENTS! WE BOTH SUFFER FROM...

ANORAKNOPHOBIA!!

DEREK!

YES???

IT'S ERIC, ACTUALLY.

YOU'RE LUCKY MR PATEL BROKE YOUR TRANCE. YOU COULD HAVE BEEN PERMANENTLY BRAINWASHED.

NOW YOU'RE FREE YOU CAN HELP US DEAL WITH THAT LOT.

WE'VE GOT TO CONTACT THE AUTHORITIES BUT THE HOTEL PHONES ARE DEAD.

OH. WE CAN USE THE REVOLUTIONARY NEW INVENTION I ENTERED FOR THE CONVENTION.

THAT'S NOT NEW-- THAT'S A MOBILE PHONE!

AYE. BUT DEREK'S DON'T NEED A BATTERY. IT'S CLOCKWORK...

...AND I'VE INVENTED A MOBILE KEY TO GO WITH IT!

AY UP! DERRICK'S KEY'LL WORK ON MY INVENTION; THE AUTOMATIC CLOCK WINDER THAT WINDS CLOCKS AUTOMATICALLY. ONCE YOU'VE WOUND IT UP, THAT IS. LET'S TRY.

WIND HERE

KEEP WINDING, DERRICK.

KEEP YER HAIR ON, DEREK.

WHIZZ! WHIRR! SPIN! H-E-L-P!

IF THE CONVENTION HAD GONE AHEAD, MY PING PONG -O-MATIC MIGHT HAVE HAD A CHANCE!

BREAKFAST TIME IN THE OCEANSIDE BUTTERY...

EE BAH GUM I'M NOT SURPRISED SERVICE IS SLOW THIS MORNING.

WHY'S THAT, MR PATEL?

LOOK AT THE PAPER.

NORTHERN RIVIERA ECHO
SPARROW STREET GANG GROUNDED

OH I KNOW. MR DO-IT-ALL, THE HOTEL SECURITY OFFICER, HANDED BERT AND QUEENIE TO POLICE LAST NIGHT.

NORTHERN RIVIERA ECHO
SPARROW STREET GANG GROUNDED
"I'LL MESMERISE THE LOT OF YOU" VOWS CAPTURED QUEENIE

NO. I MEAN THIS.

NORTHERN SPARROW STR. GANG GROUND I'LL MESMERISE THE LOT OF YOU! —QUEENIE

BLINKIN' NORA!

HE CAN'T QUIT NOW!

SPLENDIO HOTELIER CLAIMS MASSIVE REWARD
"I QUIT" SAYS MR DO-IT-ALL

I'M GOING TO TAKE THIS UP WITH THE HOTEL DOORMAN, RECEPTIONIST, PORTER, ROOM SERVICE OPERATIVE, LAUNDRYMAN, GARDENER, SECURITY OFFICER... AND OWNER!

SMASH! CLATTER! CRASH!

EXCUSE ME. WHERE ARE YOU GOING?

ON 'OLIDAY. PERMANENT, LIKE. I'VE 'AD ENOUGH RUNNING THIS PLACE ON ME TOD.

YOU'RE NOT GOING 'TIL I GET MY TANKTOP AND SOCKS BACK, PLEASE. PROPERLY LAUNDERED!

LAUNDRY'S OUT BACK. OH -- AND WHILE YOU'RE FETCHIN' IT...

YOU CAN 'AVE THE 'OTEL AN' ALL AND GIVE TO YER DOG. IT WAS 'IM WHAT REALLY CAPTURED THE SPARROW STREET GANG.

I BEG YOUR PARDON?

I SAID YOUR DOG CAN 'AVE THE HOTEL SPLENDIO. I'M OFF TO SPEND ME REWARD.

AN HOTEL! OF HIS VERY OWN! I WONDER WHAT GROMIT'LL SAY ABOUT THAT? PROBABLY NOT MUCH AS USUAL.

OUTSIDE THE LAUNDRY...

AT LAST! A CLEAN TANK TOP AND SOCKS, DRY AS A BONE THANKS TO A BLUSTERY NORTH-EASTERLY FORCE 5 GUSTING 6.

SQUELCH!

PESKY SEAGULLS!!

BACK HOME IN WEST WALLABY STREET, WASHDAY...

'ERE. 'AT 'OOD 'O IT.

I SAID 'THERE, THAT SHOULD DO IT.' THE WASHING MACHINE REPAIRED USING ONE PING PONG-O-MATIC -- AND THE OTHER RADICALLY REMODELLED.

C'MON. LET'S SEE IF WE CAN'T EASE THE WASHDAY BLUES AND MAKE PIGEON MENACE A THING OF THE PAST.

YOU WIND -- I'LL CRANK.

RATCHET!

RATCHET!

RATCHET!

WWHIRRRRR!

BRILLIANT, GROMIT! I DON'T THINK MR PATEL'S PIGEONS'LL COME ANYWHERE NEAR MY TANK TOPS NOW!

BIRD SEED

OH. THERE'S MR PATEL NOW. HELLO!

HELLO! THERE'S A FORCE 8 FORECAST, YOU KNOW.

ER, WELL IF IT GETS TOO BLOWY LATER, POP ROUND. WE'RE HAVING *CHEESE*.

DO YOU MEAN RIPENED DAIRY PRODUCT MADE BY SEPARATING CURDS AND WHEY WHICH, WHEN IN A STATE OF DECOMPOSITION, IS OFTEN VERY ATTRACTIVE TO *TYROPHAGUS LONGIOR* OR THE COMMON CHEESE MITE?

ER, NO. I MEAN WE'RE HAVING WENSLEYDALE.

44